Sisters

Judith Caseley

Greenwillow Books
An Imprint of HarperCollinsPublishers

**Special thanks to my models,
Sierra and Susan Estep**

Sisters
Copyright © 2004 by Judith Caseley
All rights reserved. Manufactured in China by South China Printing Company Ltd.
www.harperchildrens.com

Watercolor paints, colored pencils, and a black pen were used to prepare the full-color art.
The text type is Giovanni Bold.

Library of Congress Cataloging-in-Publication Data
Caseley, Judith.
Sisters / by Judith Caseley.
p.   cm.
"Greenwillow Books."
Summary: When Melissa's parents adopt Kika from another country,
the two girls learn about being sisters.
ISBN 0-06-051046-3 (trade). ISBN 0-06-051047-1 (lib. bdg.)
[1. Adoption—Fiction. 2. Sisters—Fiction.] I. Title.
PZ7.C2677 Sj 2004 [E]—dc21 2003049013

First Edition 10 9 8 7 6 5 4 3 2 1

 Greenwillow Books

To G.M.,
for the laughter

❧ Melissa ❧

Mama and I hear the clink of the mailbox.
We rush outside, and Mama opens a letter.
"Ohhhh!" she says, and she shows me a photo.
My new sister has arrived in the mail.
"Isn't she beautiful?" Mama says. She hangs the
picture on the refrigerator next to one of me.

Grandma Cecilia comes to stay, and Mama
and Papa go away on a trip.
"We'll bring Kika home soon," Papa tells me.

A few weeks later Grandma takes me to the
airport. We watch the airplane land.
Mama is holding a little girl with dark curly
hair. Papa lifts me up.
"Meet your new sister," Mama says.
"Did you fly through the clouds?" I ask the
little girl.
She doesn't answer.

⊰ Kika ⊱

Now I have a mother and father. Over and
over I say my new words. "Mother." "Father."
I am learning.
I wake up in the sunshine in my new room.
There are so many toys, I cannot choose.
My new sister's face appears at my pillow.
Her name is Melissa, and she smiles at me.
I am too afraid to smile back.

When I eat my breakfast, I spill my juice.
I wait to be scolded, but my mother cleans
it up. My new sister says, "I do that all the time."
The three of us take a walk together. My sister
and I run our hands along the bushes.
"This is honeysuckle," my sister says. She snaps
off the bottom and pulls on the stem. It tastes
sweet.

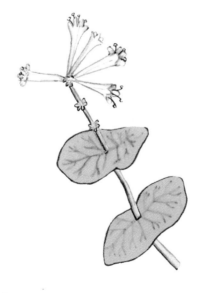

Melissa

I am teaching Kika to speak. She is quiet.
I am noisy. Sometimes she doesn't understand.
"Don't talk so fast," I tell Grandma Cecilia.
"Don't talk so loud," I tell my cousins. Now
they are Kika's cousins, too.

Mama takes us to the library.
I find five books, but Kika
can't choose. At last she gives
my mother a book.
"No more?" says Mama.
Kika says, "Just one."
Mama reads the book to us.
"A birthday party," she begins.
"What is that?" my sister says.
"You will like it," I tell her.

~Kika~

My mother takes us to the playground.

I climb up the slide and look behind me.

A girl with red curls is following.

My sister says, "We'll make a train."

We wrap our legs around each other and

slide down in a line.

"Choo choo," says Melissa.

"Choo choo," says the girl with red curls.

"Choo choo," I say, and we slide to the bottom.

Mama gives us all a snack.

Melissa says, "Cookie!" and eats one up.

Then she points to Lucy and says, "Friend!"

Cookie. Friend. Two nice new words. I eat

my cookie also.

Melissa

Lucy invites us to her birthday party, seven
days away. I tell Kika, "Soon you will see,"
and we mark the day on the calendar.
Mama wraps Lucy's present in rainbow paper,
and we make a birthday card.
I write the word *love* inside with glue, and Kika
sprinkles glitter on top.
"When is your birthday?" I ask my sister.
Kika doesn't answer.
I draw a question mark with a heart around it.

~Kika~

I do not know when I was born. I do not have a birthday. I just remember being little in a great big room with lots of children and so much noise. I miss my friends. I miss the noise. I feel afraid when the house is quiet. I'm glad my sister is not quiet.

Mama and Papa say, "I love you," before I fall asleep.

Melissa

Mama and Papa take us out to a restaurant.
Papa holds my hand, and Mama holds Kika's.
We'll change places when we walk home.
Kika asks me, "What is pizza?" I show her
a picture of it on the wall.
We watch a man roll out pizza dough and
cover it with sauce.
He gives us both a lump of dough.
We flatten the dough and draw funny faces.

I hand Mama my pizza crust.
Mama eats it and says, "Delicious."
Kika eats hers and says she likes
it, too.
"You take after Mama," I tell my
sister.
Two waiters appear with a cake
and candles.
"Surprise!" I shout, and everybody
claps.
"Today is special," Mama tells us.
"We'll call it Kika's birthday."
We sing "Happy Birthday," and
I show Kika how to blow out
the candles.
"I like birthdays," Kika says.
"I knew you would," I tell her.

Kika

When we get home, Mama and Papa give me a pretty doll with black hair just like mine. Mama says that it is just for me. I do not have to share.

My sister wants to play with it, and she starts to cry.

She cries and cries, but Papa says no.

"I don't like you anymore," says Melissa.

I don't like her, either.

"Time to go to sleep," says Mama. "Happy birthday, little Kika."

"You'll be friends again tomorrow," says Papa.

I do not think so. I cannot sleep. It is very quiet and very dark.

My sister calls from the other room, "Kika, are you awake?"

I do not answer, and she calls again. "Kika, can you hear me?"

Slippers shuffle. Melissa arrives and gives me
a picture that she has painted. It's a birthday
card. At the bottom, she has signed it "LOVE."
I know what it means. We are sisters.